Sea Sick

Ahoy, mateys!

Set sail for a brand-new
adventure with the

PUPPY PIRATES

#1 *Stowaway!*
#2 *X Marks the Spot*
#3 *Catnapped!*
#4 *Sea Sick*

Coming Soon:
Super Special #1 *Ghost Ship*

PUPPY 🐾 PIRATES

Sea Sick

by Erin Soderberg
illustrations by Russ Cox

A STEPPING STONE BOOK™
Random House 🏠 New York

For Henry, who asked me to write
him an adventure series...I hope
this one keeps you entertained
on *your* sick days, buddy.
—E.S.

Text copyright © 2016 by Erin Soderberg Downing and Robin Wasserman
Cover art copyright © 2016 by Luz Tapia
Interior illustrations copyright © 2016 by Russ Cox

All rights reserved. Published in the United States by Random House
Children's Books, a division of Penguin Random House LLC, New York.

Random House and the colophon are registered trademarks and A Stepping
Stone Book and the colophon are trademarks of Penguin Random House LLC.

Visit us on the Web! randomhousekids.com
SteppingStonesBooks.com
Educators and librarians, for a variety of teaching tools, visit us at
RHTeachersLibrarians.com

Library of Congress Cataloging-in-Publication Data
Soderberg, Erin, author.
Sea sick / Erin Soderberg. — First edition.
pages cm. — (Puppy pirates ; #4)
Summary: Captain Red Beard is too sick to organize the Pirate Day party, so it
is up to Wally and the other pirate pups to get things ready—the trouble is that
the Captain is very particular, and Wally has lost the decoder that would let
them read the instructions.
ISBN 978-0-553-51176-5 (trade) — ISBN 978-0-553-51177-2 (lib. bdg.) —
ISBN 978-0-553-51178-9 (ebook)
1. Dogs—Juvenile fiction. 2. Pirates—Juvenile fiction. 3. Parties—Juvenile fiction.
[1. Dogs—Fiction. 2. Pirates—Fiction. 3. Parties—Fiction.] I. Title.
PZ7.S685257Se 2016 [Fic]—dc23 2015014057

Printed in the United States of America
10 9
First Edition

This book has been officially leveled by using the F&P Text Level Gradient™
Leveling System.

CONTENTS

Pirate Day Prep

"*Yo ho ho and a bundle of beef! Yo ho ho and a lottle of fun!*" Captain Red Beard danced across the deck of his ship. He was singing a silly, happy tune. "*I love my ship and I love my crew, but I'm still number one!*"

None of the puppy pirates on board the *Salty Bone* was used to seeing their captain so jolly. Usually, the scraggly terrier was pretty gruff. But Captain Red Beard's favorite holiday, Party Like a Pirate Day, was just one day away.

He couldn't leash in his excitement.

"All paws on deck," the captain ordered, his tail wagging happily. "Time to prepare for our world-famous Party Like a Pirate Day banquet!"

A cuddly golden retriever pup named Wally skidded across the deck. He stood at attention. "Aye, aye, Captain," Wally barked. "I am ready to help."

"Excellent, little Walty," Red Beard said. The captain patted Wally's head with one of his scraggly paws. "Good boy."

Wally's fluffy tail swished back and forth. He loved when Captain Red Beard was pleased with him. As the newest member of the puppy pirate crew, Wally was always working hard to show the captain he deserved his bunk on board the ship. Wally's best mate, a boy named Henry, joined Wally and the dozens of other pups gathered around the captain.

"Listen up, crew!" Red Beard ordered. "Party Like a Pirate Day is tomorrow. As you all know, the Pirate Day party is absotootly the bestest event of the whole year."

The puppy pirates cheered. No one more excited than Wally. This was his first Party Like a Pirate Day. He had heard plenty of stories about past parties from his pug friends, Piggly and Puggly. Piggly spun in happy circles when she told him about the food and treats the captain saved for the party. Puggly's favorite part was getting to skip chores to play games and sing songs.

"Everything about Pirate Day has to be perfecto-nino," the captain said. "We have much to prepare. As always, my plans for the party are written in a secret code. We don't want those furball kitten pirates to find our Pirate Day plans and steal them. Aye?"

The puppy pirates all cheered again. "Aye, aye, Captain!"

Curly, the ship's first mate, stepped forward. The poufy white mini poodle whispered, "Excuse me, Captain. You do remember how to crack your codes, though . . . correct?"

"Of course I do not remember how to crack my codes, Curly!" Captain Red Beard snapped. "What would be the point of a secret code if it's not a secret? As soon as I write 'em, I forget 'em. But I have the handy-dandy code cracker right here." The captain picked up a sheet of parchment with his mouth. He unrolled it and waved it in the air.

Henry squinted to try to make out some of the words on the piece of parchment. He read aloud: *"Party Like a Pirate Day Code Sheet: Top Secret."* Henry leaned toward Wally and whispered, "Hey, mate, we should get our hands on that! I love cracking codes."

Red Beard pushed the paper to the side and continued his speech. "I hope everyone remembers the most important rule of Pirate Day. On this super-de-dooper holiday, we do everything my way. Whatever I say goes. After all, the captain is the most important part of any pirate ship, am I right?"

Curly began, "But, Captain—"

"No buts," Red Beard said, stomping. "I get to decide everything! I'm in charge, and that's final."

Curly nodded but spoke again. "Captain, it's just that the crew has a few ideas for how to make this the best Pirate Day party yet. If only you would let us—"

"Enough!" Red Beard snapped. "I wrote up the plans for the party. Your job is to follow them. Understood?" He looked around, but no one dared say anything. "Now, pups, let's see what our first order of business is." He padded over to a list of instructions that were posted on the wall. Then he glanced down at his code sheet. "First, pups, we need to blow up balloons. Fill your bodies with wind and *puff puff puff*!"

The puppies all scrambled to grab balloons. They huffed and puffed, filling balloons quicker than Henry could tie them closed. Soon they had filled a huge crate with balloons of many colors. The captain lifted a yellow balloon out of the crate. He bopped it into the air and chased after it.

Other pups did the same. There were more than a dozen balloons bopping around.

Bop.

Bop.

Pop!

The yellow balloon popped. Red Beard yelped and jumped a foot into the air.

Pop! Across the deck, a red balloon popped.

Spike, a nervous bulldog, hid from the loud noise.

Pop! A green balloon burst, and Olly the beagle howled.

Wally spotted Piggly and Puggly giggling on the other side of the deck. As usual, the pugs were making mischief. The silly pug twins had loaded up a bamboo shooter with crunchy treats and were aiming them at the balloons.

Whenever one of the treats hit a balloon, it popped.

Red Beard spotted them. "Enough!" he barked. "This is no time for your nonsense, pugs." Red Beard scanned the crowd of pups on the deck. His eyes narrowed. "Some of my pups are missing," he growled. "Where is Steak-Eye?"

Wally looked around, searching for the ship's cranky cook.

Curly stepped forward. "Sir, Steak-Eye is feeling ill."

"Ill? What do you mean?" Captain Red Beard growled, searching the crowd again. "And Old Salt?"

"Also sick," Curly said. "There's a bug going around—sneezy noses and the stomach flea. It's taken down half the crew. Otis and Marshmallow and Paco and Puck and—"

"A *bug*?" Captain Red Beard shrieked.

"What kind of bug? We will fight it! Puppy pirates are larger and stronger than fleas. We can take it out lickety-split!"

"Not a *bug* bug, Captain," Curly gently explained. "They're sick. Unwell."

Red Beard howled. "Sickness is not allowed on Party Like a Pirate Day! Only partying! That is an order! It—it—it—it—"

Captain Red Beard's nose twitched. His whiskers trembled. His eyes squeezed shut. He sniffled. He snuffed. And then, with a mighty *ah-choo,* Captain Red Beard sneezed.

Sneezy Wheezy
Captain Queasy

"Ohhhhhh," Captain Red Beard groaned. "My head. My tongue. My paws. My nose. Everything hurts." He sneezed. He wheezed. He whined. He moaned.

The captain was tucked into bed under a heavy green blanket. Curly, Wally, Henry, and the pugs crowded around him. "What can we do for you, Captain?" Curly asked. "How can we help you feel better?"

Wally could see that Curly was sick, too—sick with worry. With the captain stuck in bed, the ship was now Curly's to run. But with the Pirate Day party to prepare, and half the crew sick in bed, *and* the usual pirate ship tasks, Wally guessed Curly was nervous about getting everything done. Wally knew she could do it. The poodle was smart and fierce, and the whole crew trusted her.

"Ice," Red Beard wheezed. "Fresh ice and the blue blanket. I like the blue blankie."

Wally ripped the green blanket off the captain's body. Curly tucked him in again—this time with the blue blanket. "Better?"

"Red. It's actually the red blanket I like," Red Beard whined.

But once he was tucked into the red blanket, he didn't like that one, either. Next it was blue again, then green, red, polka dot, black fleece, fur. . . . Finally, the captain settled on a purple-and-gold plaid blanket. He took a deep, wheezing breath. "Party Like a Pirate Day will be ruined," the captain sobbed. "The best day of the year. I've waited three hundred and ninety-two days since the last Pirate Day!"

"You mean three hundred and sixty-five?" Curly said gently. "Pirate Day comes around once a year. That's every three hundred and sixty-five days, Captain."

"As I was saying, I have waited three hundred and sixty-five days for this. And now, sick!" Red Beard cried. "Sick with the sneezies and a stomach flea. What will we do?"

"You need not worry, Captain," Curly said. "As your trusty first mate, I will make sure the ship is ready for the party tomorrow."

"Impossible!" Red Beard sneezed, then wiped his drippy nose on the blanket. "I'm the only one who can do it. Without me in charge, Pirate Day is ruined."

"It's not!" Wally yelped. He hated to see the captain so upset. "Curly can do it. And we'll all help her."

"Listen to the little pup," Curly told the captain. "I can handle this."

The captain's eyes drooped. He was nearly asleep. "You promise?"

"You can count on us, Captain." Curly looked to Wally and the others. They all nodded. "We'll follow your orders and throw you the best Pirate Day party ever."

Captain Red Beard sighed. "I don't see how that's possible. But you can try." He reached his muzzle under the blanket and grabbed something in his teeth. "Here is my Party Like a Pirate Day Top-Secret Code Sheet. You can use it to decode my instructions. But please, keep it safe. It's the only copy."

"Of course," Curly said. "We'll get to work right away."

"Arrrrr!" Captain Red Beard cried out suddenly. "I have an itch!"

"Where?" Curly asked, dropping the code sheet to the floor. "Would you like me to scratch it for you before I go?"

Red Beard whimpered. "Yes. My ear. The lefty one."

Curly used her paw to scratch at the captain's ear. After a good, long scratch, she hopped off his bed and made her way toward the door. "Crew, follow me. We must get to work on the party plans at once."

"Curly?" Red Beard croaked. "Please don't go. Stay with me. What if I need something?"

Wally stepped forward. "Sir, I could stay here and take care of you. Curly has a crew to run and a ship to steer."

14

"And Piggly and I would be happy to start working on the party," said Puggly. She shot her sister a sly look.

Captain Red Beard burrowed under his covers and whined. "But I need Curly. She's my first mate. I must have her by my side." He looked at Curly with his saddest puppy-dog eyes. "Please?

You can run the ship and plan the party from here."

Curly sighed. "If you need me, I'll stay."

The captain yawned, then fell fast asleep. Curly turned to the others. "Wally, take the captain's code cracker. Guard it carefully."

Wally barked, "Aye, aye, Substitute Captain Curly!" He gently picked up the piece of parchment with his mouth. Then he and Henry and the pugs ran up to the deck.

As they ran, Wally barked "ahoy" at another pup—and that's when it happened. The wind came out of nowhere and tugged the code sheet from his mouth. It fluttered across the deck. Wally and Henry lunged for it, but another gust of wind pulled it out of reach. In a blink, it floated up and over the side of the ship.

Wally and his friends stared out at the ocean, eyes wide. The vast blue sea stretched for miles on every side of the ship. Somewhere among

those dark, frothy waves was a piece of parchment. A piece of parchment Wally was told not to lose, no matter what. It had been an accident. But would the captain and Curly see it that way? Wally didn't think so.

Party Like a Pirate Day was ruined. And it was all his fault.

Crack a Code

"In case you were wondering?" Henry said. "I think we might be in some serious trouble."

Puggly snorted. "You think?" She sneezed, spun in a circle, and sat down. "The captain's code sheet is gone!"

"All right, mates," Piggly said as she chewed on one of Henry's old boots. Piggly was always eating something. "Let's figure this out: how can we get the ship ready for Pirate Day if we don't have the captain's code cracker?"

"Yeah," Puggly said. "The captain wants things done his way. If we don't do it right, we'll all be walking the plank."

The four friends trotted over to the list of instructions posted on the wall. None of the captain's codes made any sense. It was just a mess of letters and numbers.

"Maybe we should tell Curly?" Piggly suggested. "She would know what to do."

"We can't tell Curly," Wally said. "She might tell the captain." Wally thought for a moment. "We're just going to have to crack the captain's codes ourselves."

Wally stared at the captain's list of Pirate Day orders. The first instruction made no sense at all:

STEP 1: DECORATIONS

P	B	A	O	B	L;	N	O
A	A	I	O	E	D	T	R
I	N	N	R	C	O	T	S.
N	N	T	S.	A	N'	H	
T	E	T	J	R	T	E	
T	R	H	U	E	P	F	
H	S,	E	S	F	A	L	
E	P	D	T	U	I	O	

"Pibabel no?" Henry said, trying to read the words from left to right.

"Pibabel no!" Piggly echoed. "Yes, let's do that! But . . . what is that?"

The pups on deck all stepped forward to look at the strange words on the page. No one could figure out what they meant.

Henry scratched his head as he stared at the jumble of letters. "Here's the thing about secret codes," he said, pressing his finger to the paper.

"They aren't meant to make sense when you look at them the first time. We have to try to read it in an unusual way."

"Maybe we're supposed to read this backward?" Wally said.

"Oh, I you tadeepee!," Puggly sounded out. "Nope, don't think so."

Henry didn't say anything. He ran his finger up and down the lines of letters, then gasped. "Look! If you read the words from the top down, they make sense."

P B A O B L, N O
A A I O E D T R
I N N R C O T S.
N N T S. A N' H
T E T J R T E
T R H U E P F
H S, E S F A L
E P D T U I O

"*Paint the banners, paint the doors. Just be careful, don't paint the floors,*" Henry whooped.

"Of course!" Puggly cheered. "We're supposed to paint the ship to make it look pretty. I'll get the purple paint. And glitter!" Puggly loved fancy things.

"Green," Piggly argued. "The captain's favorite color is green."

"I thought it was red," yelped Puggly. "Like the color of his reddish fur."

Wally yipped to get their attention. "The captain is sick, so we can't ask him. We just have to pick our favorite colors and get started. Hopefully, Captain Red Beard will like it."

Wally got the rest of the crew up on deck to help them, while Piggly and Puggly found the paints. Then everyone got started. Wally and Henry worked on painting all the doors on the ship different colors. Other pups rolled out long pieces of paper and painted banners that said: *Yo ho ho for Pirate Day!* and *Three Cheers for Captain Red Beard!* and *Beware the Salty Bone!* So many pups were in bed with the stomach flea that the few who were well had to work extra hard.

But the pugs thought that extra work deserved extra play. And with no one in charge, it was so tempting to goof off! Giggling, Puggly filled her pug cannon with glitter and blasted golden sparkles all over the deck. The glitter stuck to the wet paint, making the ship look like a disco ball.

Piggly didn't like to miss out on any kind of

fun. So she dipped her paws in her paint bowl and trotted across the deck. Tiny pug prints soon made curlicues across the floors.

Then the naughty sisters both sat in pans of paint, covering their tails and bottoms with color. Afterward, they sat on the banners and giggled at the marks they left behind.

Wally barked out a warning. "The captain's orders said to be careful *not* to paint the floors, Piggly. Curly is going to be really upset!"

"Eh, Curly doesn't scare me," Piggly huffed. "She's not the captain. She's just the substitute captain. What's the worst that could happen?"

"Yeah, stop being so serious, Wally!" Puggly snatched Wally's paintbrush out of his mouth. She leaped to the other side of the deck with it.

"Give that back!" Wally begged.

"Come and get it," Puggly teased. She pressed her front paws flat, poked her rear end up in the air, and wagged her tail. "Wanna play chase?"

Wally knew he should keep working. But chase was his *favorite*. He couldn't resist. Puggly dashed madly from one side of the deck to the other with the paintbrush tight in her teeth. Wally chased after her. Olly and Spike chased after him—and soon everyone was playing instead of working!

The pups tumbled and rolled back and forth across the deck. They knocked over paint cans and slid through puddles of paint. Before long, the whole floor was covered in thousands of colorful paw prints, swerving this way and that.

Everyone was having a blast. And then:

Ding ding ding!

The sound of a far-off bell rang through the air. Everyone froze.

"Avast!" A tiny bark cut across the deck. It was Curly. She growled at the crew, who were covered in paint and sparkles. "What is the meaning of this?"

Ring! Ding!
Dong! Honk!

"Well?" Curly stamped her little paw in a puddle of paint. "What's going on here?"

Henry ducked behind a banner. Spike shook with worry. Piggly and Puggly lay down to hide their paint-covered feet and bottoms.

Wally panted, trying to catch his breath. "Uh, just doing a little painting?" he said. "These are our decorations for the party. Following the captain's orders!"

Curly took in the orange and yellow ship

rails, the floor full of pink and purple paw prints, and the glitter that covered *everything*. "This is what the captain's instructions said?" she asked. "Really?"

"Paint the banners, paint the doors . . ." Wally decided to leave out the part about being careful not to paint the floors. They had a little cleaning to do before the captain was back up and at 'em. Luckily, he and Henry were experts at swabbing the deck.

"How's the captain feeling?" Puggly asked. A drop of pink paint slid down her ear and splatted on the floor.

"He's snoozing," Curly said. "I wanted to make sure everything was going okay. Captain Red Beard is so worried about Pirate Day. This is my chance to show him he can trust me to keep everything rolling right along without him."

"Everything's fine," Wally said quickly. Sure,

he'd lost the secret code sheet. But they hadn't had any trouble cracking the captain's first code, had they? He was pretty sure they could figure out the rest of the captain's instructions. All they needed was a little time. "Just taking a quick break for a game of fetch. Want to join us?"

Ding ding ding!

Curly jumped. "That's the captain's bell," she explained. "I tied a little bell around his neck. Told him if he needed anything, he could ring for me."

Dong dong dong!

Another bell sounded, deeper and quieter than the first. The pups all pricked up their ears.

Ring-a-ling-ling! A third bell, followed quickly by . . .

Honk! A horn. Spike hid behind an overturned crate.

"What is that honking?" Henry wrinkled his nose and looked all around. "There aren't any geese on board our ship. At least, I don't think there are. . . ."

Curly closed her eyes and took a deep breath. "I gave Old Salt and Steak-Eye bells, too. Marshmallow has a horn. I ran out of bells. There weren't enough for all the sick pups."

Ring-a-ling-ling!
Ding ding ding!
Honk! Honk! Honk!
Dong dong dong!

Bells and horns rang out from all corners of the ship. It sounded like every sick puppy on board needed something.

And they needed it *now.*

"I'm *coming!*" Curly howled. She looked frazzled. "Everyone wants something, and the captain wants *everything.* I'm just one pup. What am I supposed to do?"

Wally looked at the paint-splattered ship and thought about how much cleaning they had to do. And how many Pirate Day codes they still had to crack.

Then he looked at Curly, who seemed like she had *had it*. The bells got louder and louder. The horn honked without stopping.

Curly wasn't the only one who wasn't sure what to do.

"Party planning can wait," Wally said suddenly. They would crack the codes later. Curly needed him. The captain needed him. "Nurses Wally and Henry, reporting for duty."

Is It Ready Yet?
Is It Ready Yet?

"Captain?" Wally said quietly. He pushed open the door to Red Beard's quarters. Henry trailed behind him. "You rang?"

Ah-choo!

The captain sneezed. He dug feebly at his covers, trying to carve out a comfortable spot in his sickbed. "I need a snack," he whined. "My tummy is sore."

"What sounds good, Captain Red Beard?" Wally asked.

"Sardines," the captain whispered. "With pink jam."

"Strawberry jam, sir?"

"Pink!" Red Beard growled. "Pink-flavored jam, Walty. None of this hairy berry bumbo *fruit* business."

Wally nodded. "You got it, Captain. Sardines with pink jam." He hustled out of the room, Henry on his heels.

The moment he closed the door, the captain's bell rang.

Ding ding ding!

Wally peeked back into the captain's quarters. "You rang?"

"Is it ready yet?" Captain Red Beard asked weakly.

"Not yet, sir. I just need to run up to the galley to make it. Since Steak-Eye is sick, I'll have to prepare it myself." He crept toward the door again, then turned. "But I'll be back in just a minute, Captain. Promise." He raced out the door.

Ding ding ding! The captain hollered, "*Now* is my snack ready, Walty?"

Wally peeked through the door again. "Nope," he said. "Not quite yet, sir."

"What's taking so long?" Captain Red Beard whined.

Wally sighed. Captain Red Beard wasn't the easiest patient on the seven seas.

Before Wally could dash off to the galley, Henry stopped him. He said, "Hey, mate? I'm gonna head up to the main deck again. I want to take another look at the captain's list of Pirate Day instructions. In case you were wondering, we have a few more codes to crack before everything will be ready for the big day!"

Wally barked his agreement. Henry's idea to split up was a good one. At the rate they were moving, they would not be ready for the Party

Like a Pirate Day party. Henry could get to work on the next code while Wally prepared the captain's snack. They made such a great team.

Henry raced up the stairs to the main deck, and Wally ran toward the galley.

Inside the ship's kitchen, Wally found Piggly munching her way through a box of treats while she got a juicy steak ready for Old Salt. She had spilled snacks everywhere.

Curly was warming up a hot-water bottle for Steak-Eye. In the process, a lot of the water had ended up on the floor.

Spike was getting a soft cloth to clean a soup spill off Marshmallow's fur. As he made his way around the kitchen, Spike kept knocking piles of dishes onto the floor. Other dishes were piled high in the sink, waiting to be washed.

Wally tossed a stack of sardines into the first clean dog dish he found. Then he plopped a clump of pink jam on top of the tiny fish. He didn't even have time to put away the jam as he raced the sardines back to the captain's side.

"What is this?" Red Beard coughed. His tongue lolled out of his mouth.

"Your snack, sir."

Ding ding ding!

Wally hid his head under his paws to try to block out the noise. "What do you need now, sir? I'm right here. You don't need to ring the bell."

"I don't like the look of this snack," Red Beard announced.

Wally cocked his head. "But, sir, it's sardines with pink jam. Just what you asked for."

"I want it in my special dish. One of the golden bowls I save for Pirate Day." Red Beard pouted. "Put my snack in a gold dish so it will taste better."

"Aye, aye, Captain," Wally said, running from the room again. He found the captain's special dishes buried under a lot of kitchen clutter. He dumped the sardines and pink jam into a shiny gold bowl and hustled back to Red Beard's sick-bed. "Is this the dish you like, Captain?"

Red Beard pressed his nose to the snack and sniffed. He groaned. "It's too cold. And I like the jam *under* the sardines. It tastes better that way."

"Right-o," Wally said, running out of the room again. He warmed the sardines over a fire in the galley, then plopped them on top of the pink jam. "This should do it," he muttered.

But when he presented the plate to the captain, Red Beard moaned. "Forget it," he said sadly, pushing the dish aside. "I'm not really

hungry anymore. Thanks anyway, little Walty."

Wally sighed. "Is there anything else you need, Captain?" He tried not to think about how much time he had spent getting the captain's snack ready—time he *could* have spent getting the ship ready for the Pirate Day party.

Red Beard nodded. "I need someone to cuddle with. Fetch my stuffed duck!"

Wally grabbed the duck from a basket in the corner and placed him beside Captain Red Beard. The sick captain curled around his stuffed buddy, then fell fast asleep.

As soon as Wally was sure it was safe to move again, he crept out of the room. He tiptoed down the hall quietly, hoping his needy captain would stay asleep for a very long time!

Nummer Yummers

When Wally finally got back up to the main deck, most of the puppy pirates were gathered around the captain's list of instructions. Now that the patients had all been cared for, the others could get back to work. There wasn't much time left.

Curly was off meeting with Chumley, the German shepherd who ran the map room. The two of them were making sure the ship was on course for calm seas. No one wanted to hit a storm before the Pirate Day party!

"What's the next thing on the instructions list?" Wally asked Piggly.

Through a mouthful of cheese and bacon treats, Piggly blurted, "We dun dough."

"You don't know?" Wally guessed. He tried to squeeze through the crowd to get to Henry. When he was near enough to see the codes, Wally's first thought was that the next one was much trickier than the last:

STEP 2: NUMMER YUMMERS

20 18 5 1 20   20 9 13 5,
13 5 1 20   20 9 13 5,
12 15 20 19   15 6   25 21 13 13 25
5 1 20   20 9 13 5.
16 5 5 11   21 14 4 5 18   20 8 5
16 5 16 16 5 18!

"Blimey. This code is in some other language," Spike said, whimpering. "We'll never figure it out. Never, never, never."

"Never say never," Puggly scolded. "A pirate can do anything if she sets her mind to it."

Henry chewed on his lower lip and stared at the jumble of numbers. "It says 'nummer yummers' at the top, so maybe this code is telling us something about the food for the party."

"Aye," Wally barked. He loved that his best mate was so smart about everything.

"In case you were wondering," Henry said, "I think it might be some sort of recipe."

"I doubt that," Piggly said. Crumbs toppled out of her mouth. "The captain can't cook."

Henry began writing something on the bottom of the list of instructions. It was the alphabet. Under each letter, he wrote a number.

A	B	C	D	E	F	G	H	I	J	K	L	M	N
1	2	3	4	5	6	7	8	9	10	11	12	13	14

O	P	Q	R	S	T	U	V	W	X	Y	Z
15	16	17	18	19	20	21	22	23	24	25	26

"It's a letter-to-number code!" Henry said, slapping his hand to his forehead. One by one, he put a letter under each of the numbers on Red Beard's list.

20 18 5 1 20   20 9 13 5,
T R E A T   T I M E,

13 5 1 20   20 9 13 5,
M E A T   T I M E,

12 15 20 19 15 6 25 21 13 13 25
L O T S O F Y U M M Y

5 1 20 20 9 13 5.
E A T T I M E.

16 5 5 11 21 14 4 5 18 20 8 5
P E E K U N D E R T H E

16 5 16 16 5 18!
P E P P E R!

"See?" Henry said, grinning at the gathered crew. "It says: *Treat time, meat time, lots of yummy eat time. Peek under the pepper!* The captain must have hidden our special treats for Pirate Day. This tells us where to find them!"

"Follow me," Piggly ordered. She led the crew toward the galley. "I know my way around the kitchen!"

But when they arrived in the galley, everyone screeched to a halt. Dishes were everywhere, and food scraps littered the floor. Nothing was in its usual place. With Steak-Eye sick in bed, no one had done dishes since dinner the night before. Pups had been in and out of the kitchen all day, helping themselves to snacks.

The place was such a mess that it took a few moments before they noticed Steak-Eye, the ship's tiny cook, spinning in lazy circles in the center of the room. A blanket draped across his back dragged along the floor.

"Steak-Eye!" Wally gasped.

The cook looked at him with watery, sleepy eyes. *Ah-choo!*

"Are you okay?" Piggly asked.

Steak-Eye blinked twice, spun in one last circle, then curled up and fell fast asleep.

"Is he . . . sleepwalkin'?" Spike wondered.

Steak-Eye snored loudly. Then he made a *glug-glug-glurrgh* noise in his sleep.

"Don't laugh," Puggly warned. "We don't wanna wake him. He'll be furious if he wakes up and sees the state of his kitchen!"

While a few pups worked together to carry Steak-Eye back to his quarters, Henry said, "I wonder who made such a mess of this place?"

"I came in to get Old Salt a snack earlier," Piggly explained. "And I fixed a couple midnight snacks for myself last night."

"I got some sardines and jam for the captain," Wally mumbled. "But I forgot to clean up after."

"And I tried to whip up some stew for my breakfast," Spike said. "Not tasty. We need Steak-Eye to get well soon. I'm starvin'."

It was clear that almost everyone on board had been a part of making the mess in the galley. Each of the pups' little messes added up to one big mess. It was going to be impossible to find the treats for the party! Still, they got to work searching. They sniffed in pots and tore through cupboards. Soon the kitchen was even more of a mess than it had been before, and still no one could find the pepper.

Wally sniffed at the air. His nose tickled. He almost sneezed—he was pretty sure he had just picked up a whiff of pepper. It was coming from behind a towering stack of pots. He poked his nose into the stack.

It wiggled.

It wobbled.

It swayed.

Crash!

The whole stack of pots fell to the floor with a loud clatter.

"Shiver me timbers!" Henry shouted joyfully. He pushed aside the mess of fallen pots and uncovered a box marked PEPPER. The puppy pirates nosed the pepper aside. Henry lifted open the crate below. "It's full of sausages and smoked fish! This must be the captain's party food. Consider this code *cracked*!"

The puppies all cheered. But their celebration was short-lived. Curly had just walked through the door—and the galley had never been more of a disaster.

Old Salt Says

Henry leaped across the mess and tried to block Curly's view of the kitchen. "In case you were wondering, we have everything under control in here."

Curly peered between Henry's legs. "Under control?" she barked. "You call this mess *under control*?"

All the dogs backed away from her. When Curly was mad, her voice could get *very* loud.

But when she finally spoke again, Curly did not shout. Instead, the first mate sounded very calm. "Half our crew is sick with sneezy noses and the stomach flea. The deck is filled with paint. The galley is a disaster. From what I can tell, things are *not* under control. In fact, we are not much closer to being ready for the Pirate Day banquet than we were this morning. We have until tomorrow to get this ship ready for the captain's favorite day of the year. I trusted all of you to help me." She looked around and shook her head sadly. "You let me down. You let the captain down."

Wally tucked his tail between his legs.

Curly sat and sighed. "This will be the first Pirate Day with no party. I guess I need to find some way to break the news to the captain."

No one said anything. It was terrible when Curly was angry. But somehow this was worse.

She was disappointed in them.

Ding ding ding!

Dong dong dong!

Ringing bells echoed from down the hall.

"Well." Curly took a deep breath. "Sounds like Captain Red Beard and Old Salt both need help again. I will tend to the captain. Could someone else check on Old Salt?"

"I will, Curly," Wally offered. "But first, do you want me to come with you to tell the captain about the party? It's not your fault the day is ruined."

Curly shook her head. "No, I'll tell him myself in the morning, after he's had a good night's rest. It was my job to make sure everything sailed right along on his sick day. I must take the blame."

Curly's shoulders sagged. She turned and slunk out of the kitchen.

Wally padded down toward Old Salt's quarters with his tail between his legs. His ears drooped. He felt terrible about disappointing Curly—not to mention the captain.

Old Salt's bell rang again, and Wally sped up. He wasn't going to disappoint anyone else today. Maybe he couldn't fix the party mess, but he could at least help his favorite Bernese mountain dog.

And, just maybe, wise Old Salt could help him, too.

Wally poked his nose into the room. "Ahoy. How are you feeling?"

Old Salt peeked at Wally from under a pile of blankets. He sneezed.

Ah-choo!

"I've felt better, kid," he wheezed. "How are things going up on deck? Everything coming along for Captain Red Beard's big Pirate Day party?"

Wally hung his head. "Not really," he admitted. "We messed up. Now everything is ruined."

"I'm sorry to hear that," Old Salt grunted. "I guess when the cat's away, the mice will play."

Wally cocked his head, confused. "We're dogs," he reminded Old Salt. "Not cats."

Old Salt began to laugh. The chuckle turned to a cough, then a sneeze. *Ah-choo!*

"Aw, Wally, boy," Old Salt chuckled. "That's just an ol' saying. It means, with the captain gone, maybe everyone is goofin' off a little more than they should."

"Oh!" Wally said, giggling. "That makes sense. Yes, that's it. Curly's the substitute captain, but it's not the same. She's so busy taking care of the captain and steering the ship and everything else. There's no one to tell us what to do."

Ah-choo!

"Y'know, Wally . . ." Old Salt hacked up a hair ball. "Bein' on a pirate crew isn't just about following your captain's orders. There's a pirate code, kid."

"I know all about codes," Wally said. "The captain wrote all the Pirate Day plans in code. We've been trying to crack them so we can figure out how to get the ship ready for the party."

"That's not the kind of code I'm talking about, Wally." Old Salt coughed. "*Code* can also mean *rules,* kid. There are rules that a good pirate needs to follow. We help each other out— that's our way. If our captain is busy with other stuff, we've gotta steer our own ship. We need to take responsibility." He coughed again. "Sometimes, Wally, you have to be your *own* captain."

Sneaky Shadows

When Wally left Old Salt's side, it was long past bedtime. Everything on board the *Salty Bone* was silent and still, except the captain's snoring. The rolling ocean waves made gentle splashing sounds as they licked at the sides of the big wooden ship.

Everyone, it seemed, was tucked in tight—patients and all. Other than Wally and the night-watch pups, only Curly was still awake. She was skittering around the ship to check on everyone and make sure things were running as smoothly as possible.

Wally couldn't stop thinking about what Old Salt had said. And he couldn't stop thinking about the Pirate Day party. Maybe Curly had given up on the party. Maybe *everyone* had given up. But Wally couldn't.

He was the one who had lost the code cracker in the first place. He'd started this whole mess. And now he was going to be the one to fix it.

Somehow.

Wally stopped in his room. He hopped up into Henry's bunk and tugged at the boy's pajamas. Henry opened his eyes and popped out of bed. "Is something wrong, mate?"

"Everything's wrong," Wally barked. "But we're going to do something about it. Just like the pirate code says." He barked again, urging Henry to follow him.

Keeping quiet so as not to wake anyone else on board, Wally led his best mate up to the deck. The moon lit their way.

As they crept toward the list of instructions, Wally realized that he and Henry were not alone. There were shadows moving near the captain's Pirate Day list.

Two short shadows.

Piggly and Puggly were slinking around the deck. The two pugs were always full of mischief. What could they be up to?

"Wally!" Piggly barked. She looked surprised to see him.

Puggly whipped her cape. She was trying to hide something under it.

"What is that?" Wally demanded.

"Nothin'," Puggly snarled.

"It's not nothing," Wally said. He drew closer. "Show me."

"You're not the captain," growled Puggly. "You can't make me."

"No, I can't make you," Wally said, thinking about his conversation with Old Salt. Surely the pugs knew about the pirate code, too. "I just want to know what you're up to. Henry and I came up here to figure out the rest of the captain's Pirate Day codes."

"You mean you still want to try to make the party work?" Puggly asked.

"Not just try," Wally said. "We're *going* to make it happen. Will you help?"

Before Puggly could answer, her cape slipped and something yellow popped out. Wally gasped. "Is that a balloon?"

"Maybe it is, maybe it isn't," Piggly snapped.

"What are you doing with the Pirate Day balloons?" Wally asked. He thought back to how Piggly and Puggly had spent the morning popping the party balloons while everyone else blew them up. Then they had fooled around with the paint while the other pups were decorating. And in the galley, they had snacked while everyone else searched for the party food. Wally sighed. "Don't you want the party to be perfect?"

Piggly and Puggly sniffed. "Of course we do. But it won't be, no matter what we do."

"What are you talking about?" Wally asked.

"With the captain sick, and Curly busy . . . well, it's never going to be the perfect party that the captain wanted," snuffled Puggly. "That's impossible without him telling us exactly what to do."

"That doesn't matter!" argued Wally. "We can figure it out for ourselves. We need to be the captains of our own ships!"

"But there are only a few dinghies on board our ship, Wally," Piggly noted. "Not enough that we can all have one of our own."

Wally shook his head. "What I mean is, we have to take responsibility for the party *without* being told exactly what to do." He cocked his head at his pug friends. "Now, are you going to help me—or are you going to stay out of the way?"

Piggly grinned at Puggly, then said, "What do you think we were doin' up here, Wally? Goofin' off?"

"Um, yes?" Wally said.

Puggly snorted. "No way, mate. You think you're the only one trying to save Party Like a Pirate Day?"

"But you just said it was impossible!" Wally pointed out.

Puggly grinned. "I said it was impossible to make this party turn out exactly the way the captain wanted it."

"So we're not going to do that," Piggly said, giggling. "We're going to make it even better."

"How?" Wally asked. "Did you crack more of the captain's codes?"

"We'll leave the code cracking to you and your boy," Piggly said. "Me and Puggly are working on a little surprise of our own. It's gonna blow the captain away!"

Party Like a
Pirate Day

Wally tried and tried to get the pugs to reveal their surprise. But they wouldn't even give him a hint.

"You're just gonna have to trust us!" Puggly said.

The sun would come up soon, and there wasn't much time left to figure out the rest of the captain's codes. So Wally and Henry got back to work.

They took Captain Red Beard's list of instructions off the wall and brought it down to their quarters. Then they snuggled under the covers with the sheet of parchment laid flat in front of them.

The second-to-last code said:

STEP 3: DESSERT!

DLOG NI DEVRES ERA YEHT
NEHW SYAWLA DNA DLOC
TON TOH RETTEB ETSAT
STAERT

"Looks like just a bunch of random letters," Henry said.

Wally stared at the strange words. He squinted so hard the letters started to blur. Then Wally had an idea. He didn't know much about decorations or cooking, but he knew a *lot* about dessert. Maybe he could work backward.

If he could think up some great desserts, it might help him figure out the captain's code.

"Wait a second!" Wally barked. *Backward . . .* He looked closer at the code. And suddenly, it all made sense.

"The words are written backward!" Henry cried, figuring it out at exactly the same time. *"Treats taste better hot not cold and always when they are served in gold."*

"*Arrr-ooo!*" Wally howled. "I know what he's talking about. Captain Red Beard wants us to serve the banquet treats in the special gold dishes he saves for Party Like a Pirate Day. He made me serve his snack in one of those fancy dishes."

Henry didn't answer. He was already staring at the next clue, which said:

STEP 4: FUNSIES

.--. .. .-. .- — . /

.--. .- .-. — -.-. /

.-. ..- .-.. . / -. ..- —

-... . .-. / --- -. . /

.-.. --- — ... /

--- ..-. / --. .- — . ...

/ -- . .- -. ... /

..-. .. -. / ...- .. -. -. /

..-. ..- -.

"In case you were wondering, this one's easy. It's Morse code," Henry said. "That's the secret language of navy ships and spies."

"But it's just a bunch of dots and dashes," Wally noted.

"You're lucky I know so much about life at sea, mate! In Morse code, each letter of the alphabet is represented by a mix of dots and dashes. If you signal it over the radio, dots are a short sound, and dashes are long." Sitting up in bed, Henry got a pencil and paper. He wrote down all the letters, A to Z. Then he scribbled dots and dashes next to each of them.

A •—
B —•••
C —•—•
D —••
E •
F ••—•
G ——•
H ••••
I ••

J •———
K —•—
L •—••
M ——
N —•
O ———
P •——•
Q ——•—
R •—•

S •••
T —
U ••—
V •••—
W •——
X —••—
Y —•——
Z ——••

His tongue poked out the side of his mouth as he thought it through. "I've got it! This one says: *'Pirate party rule number one, lots of games means fun fun fun.'* Huh."

"What?" Wally asked.

"It doesn't say what *kind* of games," Henry pointed out.

"Maybe the captain wants us to figure that out for ourselves," Wally realized. He wagged his tail. He felt like he'd just cracked the most important code of all: the pirate code!

Henry yawned. "Here's what I'm thinking, mate. I think we do our best to make the Pirate Day party as fun as we can. We might not know how to do things *exactly* as the captain had planned, but it will be a blast, no matter what!"

Wally couldn't have said it better himself. And he knew Piggly and Puggly agreed. Wally curled up beside his best mate, falling asleep almost instantly. Being his own captain was exhausting work.

At first light, Henry and Wally jumped out of bed. They had so much to do before the party. Curly was still running around helping the captain. But all the other puppies reported for duty. "We have a lot of messes to clean up,"

Wally told the crew. "And a lot of party to plan. And no one's going to tell us how to do it. So let's figure it out for ourselves!"

Spike raised a trembling paw. Wally could tell he had an idea but was afraid to say it out loud in front of all these pups.

Spike was afraid of pretty much everything.

"What is it, Spike?" Wally asked.

"I think I know how we can fix the mess we made with the paint," Spike said nervously. "We could, um, paint *more* paw prints on the deck. They could lead puppies to different parts of the party."

"It will be like the dotted lines on a treasure map!" Wally yelped. "Follow the prints to find fun, games, and food."

Everyone loved this idea, and several pups got to work with paint-filled paws.

"I'll take charge of the galley!" Piggly said. She led a group of pups down to start cleaning

things up. But there wasn't enough time to clean all the dishes before the party.

Piggly thought for a second. "We can serve the fish in golden bowls," she said. "But I have a fun new idea for how to serve the captain's special sausages, mates!" She barked excitedly. "We can stab 'em with swords and serve 'em up like shish kebabs!"

On deck, Puggly raced around with stream-

ers and bows, making everything look even more festive. Henry scrambled up on railings and helped her reach all the high corners. Soon every inch of the ship was decorated for Party Like a Pirate Day!

While the crew painted and polished and cooked and cleaned, Wally had a job of his own to do.

The most important job of all.

He had to stop Curly from telling the captain that Pirate Day was canceled. He high-tailed it to the captain's quarters, hoping he wasn't too late.

Captain Red Beard was sitting up in bed, looking much better than he had the day before. Much better . . . and *much* angrier. "What do you mean, Pirate Day is canceled?" Red Beard growled.

Uh-oh.

Curly was sitting at the foot of his bed. "I tried my best, Captain, but things got a little out of control. I just couldn't—"

Before she could say anything more, Wally laughed a loud, fake laugh. "Wasn't that a good joke, Captain?"

"What joke?" Captain and Curly asked together.

"You know, Curly, the joke about Pirate Day

being canceled. You were just playing a funny little prank on Captain Red Beard, right?"

"You were?" the captain asked.

Curly hesitated. "I was?"

"Of course you were," Wally said. "But I came down here to tell you that everything's ready for the party. So if you're feeling better, Captain Red Beard, it's time."

The captain leaped out of bed. He shook his body to fluff up his fur. It had gotten matted during his sick day in bed, and one of his ears was pressed flat to his head. "Well, what are we waiting for?" He trotted up the stairs. Wally and Curly followed close at his heels.

Curly looked at Wally, confused. "I don't understand," she whispered. "The last time I checked in, you were all goofing off. No one was getting anything done—"

Before Wally could explain, Captain Red

Beard stepped out into the sunshine. Streamers fluttered in the wind. Paw prints filled the deck. Food was piled high on platters and speared on swords and—of course—heaped inside the captain's special golden dishes. Balloons hung from the rails.

The captain's mouth fell open. "Wh-what—" he stuttered. His voice boomed. "What in the name of Growlin' Grace have you done to my party?!"

Puggy Piñatas

"Everything is so different!" Red Beard shouted.

Wally held his breath. The rest of the crew lowered their heads in fear.

The captain blinked, took it all in, and yelled again, "And I *love it*!"

The puppy pirates cheered.

The captain went on in his loudest, most important voice: "My dear crew, it seems that this year—just like every year—I planned the bestest, most supertacular Pirate Day party on all the seven seas!"

"Three cheers for Captain Red Beard!" the others called out. "*Arrrr*-oooo!"

Red Beard held his head high. "I just love how you followed my directions perfectly." He sighed happily.

The puppy pirates looked at each other. No one wanted to tell the captain that not all of his instructions were so clear. At the end of the day, maybe it didn't matter anyway. The puppy pirates had pulled off a party everyone on board could enjoy. And no one had to walk the plank.

"I have one last thing to say before we get down to business." Red Beard turned to Curly. "The sneezies and stomach flea took down your mighty captain at the worst possible time. But Curly kept us afloat, and for that I must say thank you. Curly, you have proven yourself to be an excellent leader. Someday you will make a wonderful captain of your own ship."

Curly bowed. "Don't thank me for this party, Captain. Thank your crew. Especially Wally, Henry, Piggly, and Puggly. They worked extra hard to make sure the party was a success."

"But you were a great substitute captain!" Wally ruffed. "Three cheers for Curly!"

"Maybe so," Curly said, smiling. "But you lot were your own captains when you needed to be. That's the pirate code, right?"

Wally caught Old Salt grinning at him. The older dog winked.

"Right," Wally barked.

"Just to make it absotootly clear," Red Beard said, "none of you pups will ever be as good a captain as me."

"Of course." Curly laughed. "No one will ever captain a ship as well as you do, sir."

"Yes, yes. All righty, then. Who's ready to party like a pirate?" Captain Red Beard gazed at his crew. "You all have one order to follow today: Have fun!"

"Aye, aye, Captain!" The puppy pirates scattered across the deck. The rest of the afternoon, they sang, danced, chased, played, and ate like royalty.

By late in the day, the other sick puppies felt well enough that everyone was able to take part in the fun. When Steak-Eye tasted one of the shish-kebabs-on-a-sword, he glared at the pugs. "It's fine," he growled. "Kind of clever, actually. Doesn't taste as good as something I would have cooked, but I'll eat it anyway."

"Thanks, Steak-Eye." Piggly giggled. She knew this was a compliment, coming from the cranky cook.

The cook narrowed his bulging eyes and said, "I assume my galley is clean?"

Wally looked at Piggly and Puggly nervously. Puggly grinned back. "It's spick-and-span ..." Under her breath, she whispered, "... now. But shiver me timbers, you shoulda seen the state of that place yesterday."

Steak-Eye whispered back, "Aye. Good thing I was in bed all day, eh?"

As the sun was setting, Captain Red Beard barked loudly. "Okay, everyone. Game time! What game do we have first?"

Wally gasped. He and Henry had forgotten about coming up with the games! He looked at Henry and whimpered. Had they ruined the party after all?

But before he could say anything, Piggly and Puggly trotted to the front of the ship and called for everyone's attention. "Ahoy, mates! It's pug-glorious game time!" Puggly hollered.

Wally breathed a huge sigh of relief. So *this* was the pugs' big surprise.

"Who wants to be the first to try a puggy piñata?" Piggly cried.

Captain Red Beard jumped up and down. "Me! I do! Me! I love games. I love games!"

Piggly giggled. "Step right up." She offered the captain a bamboo shooter. "Aim at a balloon. If it pops, you'll find a surprise. This is our latest invention. It's a game and a prize in one! We got the idea when we were poppin' balloons and eatin' treats yesterday morning."

Red Beard looked at the balloons hanging from the deck rail. There were hundreds of them, in dozens of colors. "Any balloon?"

"Yep," Puggly snorted. "Any balloon. If it pops, you're a winner."

Red Beard shot at one of the red balloons hanging nearest him. He missed.

Wally looked at the pugs nervously. The captain would be very embarrassed if he didn't win a prize. Thankfully, after a couple tries, the balloon burst with a loud *pop!*

Treats came raining out, all across the deck. "Treats!" Captain Red Beard exclaimed. "There are treats inside the balloon!" He leaned in close to Piggly and Puggly and whispered, "This game was my idea, right . . . ?"

"Of course," Piggly said loudly. "Of course the puggy piñatas were your brilliant idea,

Captain. After all, it wouldn't be Party Like a Pirate Day without you, sir."

As the puppies fanned out across the deck to pop the rest of the puggy piñatas and find their prizes, Wally felt so very happy. He only hoped the stomach flea would stay away for a long while. It was tiring being his own captain all the time. And to tell the truth, Wally had sort of missed Captain Red Beard while he was sick in bed. He was ready for things on board the *Salty Bone* to get back to normal!

Just then, Wally felt a strange tickling in his nose. He pawed at his snout, but the tickling got worse. *Ah-choo!* A loud, forceful sneeze knocked Wally off his feet. He skidded across the floor, landing in a heap beside the pug twins.

Ah-choo! Piggly's sneeze sent her crashing into a table heaped with food.

Ah-choo! The blast of Puggly's sneeze popped another treat-filled balloon.

Ah-choo! Henry groaned and rubbed at his eyes.

Uh-oh, Wally thought as he sneezed again. It looked like normal would have to wait.

All paws on deck!

A Super Special Puppy Pirates
is on the horizon.
Here's a sneak peek at

Ghost Ship

"Thunderstorms are exciting, don't you think?"
Henry said, laying his head on his pillow.

Wally curled up near his best mate and
yawned. He was so sleepy, but he wasn't sure he
could sleep in a storm. His body shook every

time thunder rumbled. He had never liked storms. The loud noises frightened him.

Henry rubbed Wally's fluffy ears and whispered, "In case you were wondering, I love storms. There's nothing to be scared of, mate. Not lightning. Not thunder." Henry flipped over and added, "Gosh, you don't even need to worry about monsters under the bed. I'll keep you safe, mate."

Monsters under the bed? Wally yipped and whimpered. He had never worried about *those* . . . until now!

Wally snuggled close against his friend. His worries kept him awake for a long time. When he finally fell asleep, he tossed and turned. He dreamed of Growlin' Grace and ghost ships, dark skies and rolling waves.

Crrrr-ack!

Thunder and rolling waves pounded at the ship. Wally startled awake, happy to get away from the scary dream he'd been having. In his dream, Growlin' Grace's ghost had come to make him join her crew. Wally tried to settle in and fall asleep again. That's when he heard it. . . .

Ooo-ooh! Woo-ooo! Walllll-ly!

A spooky, ghostly howl filled the room. It was coming from something pale and glowing right next to Wally's bed!

Wally leaped up. His heart was racing. The creature next to the bed was white and spooky. It had an eye patch like Old Salt's, but seemed to be floating beside the bunk like a ghost. *Growlin' Grace's ghost!*

New friends. New adventures.
Find a new series . . . just for you!

BALLPARK Mysteries
FOR THE SPORTS FAN

THE DINO FILES
FOR THE ADVENTURER

Louise Trapeze
FOR THE SUPERSTAR

PIPER GREEN
FOR THE DREAMER

PUPPY PIRATES
FOR THE ANIMAL LOVER

Tuesday Tucks adventures!
FOR THE EXPLORER

Illustrations (from left to right): : © Mark Meyers; © Mike Boldt; © Brigette Barrager; © Qin Leng; © Russ Cox; © Wesley Lowe

RandomHouseKids.com